For Rosaleen
M.W.

For Dad
J.B.

Text copyright © 1991 by Martin Waddell
Illustrations copyright © 1991 by Jill Barton

First U.S. edition 1992
First published in Great Britain in 1991
by Walker Books Ltd., London.

Library of Congress Cataloging-in-Publication Data

Waddell, Martin.
The happy hedgehog band / written by Martin Waddell ;
illustrated by Jill Barton.—1st U.S. ed.

Summary: Happy hedgehogs with drums inspire the other animals
in Dickon Wood to join them in making lively music.
ISBN 1-56402-011-8
[1. Bands (Music)—Fiction.   2. Hedgehogs—Fiction.   3. Animals—Fiction.]
I. Barton, Jill, ill.   II. Title.
PZ7.W1137Hap   1992
[E]—dc20   91-71852

10 9 8 7 6 5 4 3

Printed and bound in Hong Kong by Dai Nippon Printing Co. Ltd.

The pictures in this book were done in watercolor and pencil.

Candlewick Press
2067 Massachusetts Avenue
Cambridge, Massachusetts 02140

THE HAPPY HEDGEHOG BAND

by

Martin Waddell

illustrated by

Jill Barton

CANDLEWICK PRESS

CAMBRIDGE, MASSACHUSETTS

Deep in the heart
of Dickon Woods lived
a happy hedgehog
named Harry.

Harry loved noise,
so he made a big drum
and he banged on the drum,
tum-tum-te-tum.

A hedgehog called Helen
was out in the woods.
She heard
tum-tum-te-tum
and she liked it.

So she made a drum
and went off
to join in the drumming.

And so did a hedgehog
named Norbert
and another called Billy;
they both made drums

and followed the
*tum-tum-te-tum*s,
until all of the hedgehogs
with drums
were gathered together
at Harry's.

Tum-tum-te-tum
went one drum;
that was Harry.

Diddle-diddle-dum
went one drum;
that was Helen.

Ratta-tat-tat
went one drum;
that was Norbert.

And
BOOM
went one drum;
that was Billy.

Tum-tum-te-tum
diddle-diddle-dum
ratta-tat-tat
BOOM!
Tum-tum-te-tum
diddle-diddle-dum
ratta-tat-tat
BOOM!

All the woods
were
humming
and
tumming
with drumming.

"STOP!"

cried the pheasant,
the owl and the bee,
the mole from his hole
and
a badger called Sam
and his mother
and the fox and the crow,
the deer and the dove,
the frog and the toad
and the spider
and
the dog
who was lost
in the woods.

Tum
went the band
and they STOPPED!

"We want to play too!"
said the others.
"But we haven't
got drums.
So what can we do?"
And nobody knew
except Harry.

Harry knew all
about noise.
So he said,

you can buzz,

you can hoot,

"You can hum,

you can whistle,

you can clap,

you can click,

you can pop.

We'll carry on with the drums."

And ...

they did.

And the dog
who was lost
in the woods
just danced.

Tum-tum-te-tum

diddle-diddle-dum

ratta-tat-tat

BOOM!